This book belongs to

Aubree

Timo's Garden

Victoria Allenby
Illustrated by **Dean Griffiths**

pajamapress

First published in the United States in 2016
First published in Canada in 2015

The publisher gratefully acknowledges the support of the Canada Council for the Arts and the
Ontario Arts Council for its publishing program. We acknowledge the financial support of the
Government of Canada through the Canada Book Fund (CBF) for our publishing activities.

Library and Archives Canada Cataloguing in Publication
Allenby, Victoria, 1989-, author
        Timo's garden / Victoria Allenby ; illustrated by Dean
Griffiths. -- First edition.
ISBN 978-1-927485-84-2 (bound)
        I. Griffiths, Dean, 1967-, illustrator II. Title.
PS8601.L44658T56 2015   jC813'.6   C2015-902332-7

Publisher Cataloging-in-Publication Data (U.S.)
Allenby, Victoria, 1989 -
    Timo's garden / Victoria Allenby ; illustrated by Dean Griffiths.
[48] pages : color illustrations ; cm.
Note: An illustrated index shows every flower mentioned in the story.
Summary: "When Timo signs up for the Great, Green Garden Tour, he feels pressure to make his
garden great and neglects his friends to work in it. When his friends help him avoid a disaster, he
realizes his friendships are more important than pride in his garden" – Provided by publisher.
ISBN-13: 978-1-927485-84-2
1. Friendship – Juvenile fiction. 2. Gardening – Juvenile fiction. I. Griffiths, Dean, 1967 - . II.
Title.
[E] dc23   PZ7.1.A554Ti 2015

Cover and book design—Rebecca Buchanan

Manufactured by QuaLibre Inc./Print Plus
Printed in China

Pajama Press Inc.
181 Carlaw Ave. Suite 207 Toronto, Ontario Canada, M4M 2S1

Distributed in Canada by UTP Distribution
5201 Dufferin Street Toronto, Ontario Canada, M3H 5T8

Distributed in the U.S. by Ingram Publisher Services
1 Ingram Blvd. La Vergne, TN 37086, USA

A story for Gran
—V.A.

For Jane and Pepper
—D.G.

Toadstool Corners'
Great, Green Garden Tour
Next Sunday

Do you have a great garden?
Sign up here.

Starr Swiftclaw, The Diggs

Padma Lili, 16 Swamp-Water Way

Chip & Chuck Wood, The Burrow Inn

Ratna Chitter, 1280b 3rd Tunnel SW

Lamar Drake, 3 Ripple Road

Chapter One

"**Y**ou have a garden, Timo," said Rae. "You should put it on the tour."

Timo's whiskers twitched.

"Hmm, I don't think my garden is a *great* one," he said. "But it sounds like fun. And I have a whole week to get ready." He put his name on the list.

That afternoon Timo looked around
his garden. He always felt happy here.
There was a corner full of cosmos that
waved to him when the wind blew. A
patch of pansies cheered him up on the
gloomiest days. And the row of roses
always made his heart smile.

The garden had herbs for cooking, a lawn for visiting, and a bench for sitting and daydreaming.

It was all very nice. But it could be nicer.

"I know what this garden needs," said Timo. "A plan."

Timo got his notebook. He wrote a list. Then he wrote two more.

Things I Want to Keep
- Bench
- Herbs
- Flowers
- Bird Bath

THINGS I DO NOT WANT TO KEEP
- Weeds
- Chipped paint on the gate
- Broken flowerpots
- That strange orange flower I do not remember planting

THINGS I WANT TO ADD
- More flowers
- New mulch
- ~~A patio with a barbecue and a grape arbor overhead~~
- Maybe a grape vine

12

Timo looked at his lists, thinking. He scratched an ear. He nibbled his pencil. Then he nodded. "I can make this garden great in one week. No problem."

That night Timo honed his hoe and sharpened his spade.

He sanded their handles and oiled their blades.

Then he went to bed and dreamed of violets.

On Monday Timo hopped to it with a wiggle and a giggle.

He weeded and he watered.

He hoed and he hauled.

Soon the roses seemed rosier. The marigolds were more merry.

The garden looked good. But it was not quite great.

Maybe that bush would look better over there, Timo thought. He picked up a spade.

Just then, Hedgewick poked his snout over the gate.

"Great garden!" he said. "Can I take a little parsley?"

"Of course," said Timo, digging in his spade. Soil scrunched. Gravel crunched.

Hedgewick munched a parsley sprig. "You should come over for lunch, he said. "I'm making spinach cakes."

Timo paused. Hedgewick made the best spinach cakes. But there was so much he wanted to do for his garden.

"Not today," he said. "I only have six days to get ready for the tour."

Chapter Two

On Tuesday Timo set to work with a skip and a song. He snipped the stalks and clipped the leaves. He groomed the grass and pruned the trees.

Soon the hedge was as straight as a ruler. The grass was as smooth as the fur on Timo's ears.

The garden was very tidy. But it was not quite great.

I wonder if I can prune this tree to look like a rabbit, Timo thought. He fetched a ladder.

Just then, Rae leaned over the gate. "Great garden," she said. "Are you coming to the lake with us?"

Timo was already climbing. "Sorry, Rae. I have a lot to do in five days."

Suddenly, Timo remembered that he did not like heights. He teetered and tottered on top of the ladder. His shears shook. The rungs shuddered.

"I hate to see you miss out on all of the fun," Rae called up to him.

"Oh, I am having lots of fun," Timo said, trying not to look down. "I love gardening."

Chapter Three

On Wednesday Timo began to feel rushed.

He trimmed and he tidied.

He hurried and he scurried.

He raked and he staked.

He worked and he worried.

Would he be ready in time? Would his garden be good enough?

Timo's paw tapped as he stared at the garden. There were lots of lilies. There were plenty of poppies. There were dozens of daisies. But something was missing.

I think I have just enough time to add a new flower bed, he thought. He looked around for his wagon.

Just then, Suki burst through the gate. "Timo!" she said. "Are you going to

spend *all week* in your garden? What about our tennis match?"

"Tennis?" said Timo. His gaze moved over some clover and through some rue.

"Tennis," said Suki. "We play every week."

"We play on Wednesdays." Timo eyed some irises.

"It *is* Wednesday!" cried Suki.

"It is?" Timo blinked in surprise. Then he spotted a red handle under a lilac shrub.

Suki's tail bristled. "You cannot just ignore your friends, Timo."

Timo bounded past her. His wagon bumped along behind.

"Sorry—I have to go. Time to buy flowers. Four days left!" he called.

Chapter Four

On Thursday Timo planted with a ho and a hum. His paws dragged. His whiskers sagged. Gardening was not fun anymore.

This plant was too prickly. That one was too tickly.

And the weeds grew much, much, much too quickly.

But Timo had signed up for the tour. He had made a promise. He needed a great garden by Sunday.

That afternoon Timo potted and he puttered. He mulched and he muttered. "Three more days. Three more days."

Three more days is not enough time! he thought. But he could not rush his new flowers. Gently, he planted some ginger. Gingerly, he planted some gentians.

Just then, Bogs appeared at the gate.

"Looks like rain," he said.

"Nonsense, said Timo, still scooping soil.

"If you say so," said Bogs.

Timo looked up at the cloudy sky.

"Maybe it will stop by morning," he said
hopefully.

"Maybe," said Bogs. "But probably not."

Chapter Five

On Friday it rained ALL DAY.

The wind whooshed.

The trees thrashed.

The rain rushed.

The thunder crashed.

Timo looked out the window. He could not see the flowers. He could not see the trees. He could not even see his own gate through the rain.

"And there are only two days left," Timo moaned. "I will never make my garden great in just two days."

That night Timo opened his notebook and looked at his lists. Sadly, he crossed out the grape vine. He crossed out the new coat of paint for his gate.

"Suki was right," he said. "I do not want to spend all week in my garden anymore. I do not want to care whether my garden is great or not."

But he did care. Feeling grumpy, Timo went to bed and dreamed about mud.

Chapter Six

On Saturday the garden was a mess.

The roses were mushy.

The daisies were droopy.

And the birdbath was a mud bath.

Timo started cleaning with a sniff and a sigh.

"I chose blisters and aches over cakes and lakes.

"I could have played tennis.

"I could have tended my friends instead of my garden."

I will have to say I am sorry, he thought.

While Timo clipped the roses,
he thought about the many, many,
many, many things he had to do
before the next day.

While he thought, he forgot to pay
attention.

OUCH! Timo grabbed a thorny stem
and jumped in surprise.

SQUELCH! He landed in a muddy
spot and began to fall over.

THWACK! THWACK! THWACK! His waving paw knocked over a spade, which knocked over a hoe, which knocked over a rake.

SPLAT! He landed face-first in a puddle.

"Great," Timo muttered.

Just then, Rae tapped on the gate.
"Need a paw?" she said.
"Where's the rake?" asked Suki.
"I brought lemonade," said
Hedgewick.

"They made me come," grumbled
Bogs.

Timo picked himself up, smiling as
brightly as the sun. "You are the very
best of friends," he said.

Everybody set to work.

Rae made ditches to drain the muddy puddles.

Suki raked up dripping lumps of leaves.

Hedgewick staked the sopping, flopping flowers.

Bogs even painted the old, chipped gate.

That evening Timo and his friends stood back to admire the garden.

"It looks great," said Suki.

"Are you sure?" asked Timo.

"Very sure," said Rae.

"*Great* is just the right word for it," said Hedgewick.

Timo frowned. "If only I had one more day, I would—"

"But you have no more days," said Bogs.

"I have an idea," said Rae. "After the garden tour, we should have a celebration."

"What kind of celebration?" asked Timo.

"Whatever it is, I will bring spinach cakes," said Hedgewick.

"Then I will come for sure," said Suki. "Bogs?"

"If I have to," said Bogs.

Chapter Seven

But on Sunday it rained again.

Garden Tour postponed
until next week

Timo *wilted*.

"Well," said Hedgewick, "now you have seven more days to work in your garden."

"Seven more days of weeding," said Suki.

"Seven more days of planting," said Rae.

"Seven more days of changing everything around," said Bogs.

Timo thought about his garden. He
thought about his friends.

"I know what this garden really
needs," he said.

"What?" sighed Bogs.

"A picnic," said Timo.

And it was a *great* picnic.

GLOSSARY OF FLOWERS

Clover

Cosmos

Daisy

Gentian

Ginger

Iris

Lilac

Lily

Marigold

Pansy

Poppy

Rose

Rue

Violet

46